HOSTEL ATTACK (BIGGEST BATTLE) SEASON 1

BIGGEST BATTLE (WAR)

HEMILKUMAR P PATEL

ISBN 978-93-5610-569-0

Published in India 2022 by Pencil

A brand of
One Point Six Technologies Pvt. Ltd.
123, Building J2, Shram Seva Premises,
Wadala Truck Terminal, Wadala (E)
Mumbai 400037, Maharashtra, INDIA
E connect@thepencilapp.com
W www.thepencilapp.com

DISCLAIMER: *This is a work of fiction. Names, characters, places, events and incidents are the products of the author's imagination. The opinions expressed in this book do not seek to reflect the views of the Publisher.*

Author biography

Rarely does anyone god give such an opportunity.This is an opportunity to show humanity. There is no need to be afraid here, courage is needed. Maybe even if we become martyrs, this country will think that no one can pay for the favors we have taken. The prayers of the parents of all the students join us. If we don't fight, no one will fight. We all have a chance to save, let's save everyone. Maybe one of us survives and the other survives. Let me tell you a story. : HEMILKUMAR P PATEL

CONTENTS

HOSTEL ATTACK (BIGGEST BATTLE) SEASON 1

HOSTEL ATTACK (BIGGEST BATTLE) SEASON 1

……………………………………………………………………………………

Part 1: (Seed of War)
23 March 2021

Hostel, thinking that yes, this is a great place. Three to four beds in a room, But there are tens of millions of wet memories attached to this bed. How much fun, fights in fun and if someone has a birthday,

Any student should be beaten upside down on the bed with a pillow or a belt. Then the two rooms came together, Pillows should be thrown in front of them. Turn off the lights in the dark at night and scream. To annoy the manager, To annoy someone if they are scared, Waking up the Watchmen by screaming if awake, Sometimes it is time to detonate a twine bomb.

Such is the fun of a hostel, There is talk of a hostel that was about to deteriorate.

(Future)

The main character here is Ronak who fell in a corner of the college, He had a gun in his hand. Since there was a bomb blast, It was getting dark during the day. There was black smoke all around, it will be a matter of time, He fell unconscious, It looked like the room he was in might have exploded. He suddenly regained consciousness, and began to look around. His ears were Deafness. The white shirt looked all black and blood appeared upon it. A little blood was dripping from his head. Was trying to get up, So he grabbed the wall and stood up. What would have happened now? When he went to see the room, there were corpses of all the boys in that room. Ronak went to the boy who was trembling. And he tried to talk to the boy.

"Oh, Nilesh. Wake up brother. We have to get out." Cried voice said keeping Nilesh's head in his lap.

"It's too late, you don't save me, but save the one who lives." In a hushed voice, "Now no one should die in this blast or firing, promise me." Nilesh said in a broken voice.

"Let nothing happen to everyone, You got into it. " Ronak said in reply.

Nilesh, who was covered in blood, was dead And Ronak started crying loudly. There he was in the room, there were two or three terrorists coming. Ronak was crying, then he suddenly stood up, And despite having a gun, he started hitting with his hand. Was furious, So he was beating violently, And he killed all three of them.

After Ronak, he went with Nilesh and started crying, He put his hand on his head and took out a big M-4 gun. As soon as he came in, he started beating him.

Coming in between position terrorist, Ronak started beating him. To a student who is salvaged in a different place. And proceeded with caution.

....

Part 2 : (Relationships)

Hostel life is something like that; It hurts to leave home when you come to the hostel, And it hurts to leave the hostel when the last day comes, The same is true of hostels. The highest in the world, If you want to learn with mom and dad, But this hostel is a teaching day to live without fear.

(One year before the attack)

The main character Ronak was coming to the hostel of BSG College, Ahmedabad. It's about time, The hostel was in O Sap (Civil engineer top view.), Space in centre point, Two floor, 29 room. It was morning and some people were teeth brushing outside the door. When Ronak got there, everyone was watching In front each other. Some slept leaning against the door rather than brushing, So some student get ready and walking floor, So some student learning to do something. Teaching is in the vein of the hostel student. Ronak finds his room and arrives, and opened the door, one student was dressed in the room and this got there by opening the door.

"Why did you come without asking?" Another student in that room was Nilesh, he said. (Remember that man was injured in the attack.)

"Why, You asked me to get dressed?" Ronak replied with a smile on his face.

"Oh, that's fun." Nilesh replied.

"Brother, you will have fun every day. One thing to remember, don't get me wrong, "said Nilesh.

"Now is my first day, This will be your first day in college. Meet everyone else at the hostel! " Ronak said.

"After all, Going to college right now. First to find a lovely bride, then second talk. " Nilesh said.

"Your father wouldn't have said that," Ronak said.

"Yes, whose father says so!" Nilesh said.

After all this talk, he met all the hostel students and reached the college. So he went to that class, Then a boy started running. So Ronak told him to stop but he didn't stand remained. Suddenly four or five students ran after him. Surprised situation for Ronak, Nilesh was beside him.

"Ignore, It will keep happening. This will happen on a daily basis. Because he ran ahead, He went to Sir and complained, That some student annoys him, So he got more scared, " said Nilesh.

"That's when everyone needs me." Ronak said angrily and he ran after those people. Nilesh went to

stop but he didn't stand remained. Because Ronak didn't like it.
Ronak ran to the end And in the middle of it all the rear was going to strike the front man. There came between Ronak.
"Who are you, if it's new then new remain." One student said.
"You will not scare the frightened man anymore, " said Ronak.
"Scared, What will you do?" One student said.
"I'll get rid of that fear, " Ronak said.

Quarrel in between these, the blows continue. However, the whole college and even Sir-Mem were scared of these five students. Everyone laughed when Ronak gave Sammy a chest fight. And there Ronak said, 'There is no need to be afraid of such people, Need to fight against. Once scared, to be scared until college is over. You five, Remember we are new. Organize a party for us, for freshers. But don't angry me.' Everyone said yes and the party was organized.

As far as the college is concerned, the planning of the party is well done. Enjoyed dancing and playing all the games. Ronak then thanked them all and apologized, That's it. He then explained that strength should be used in the right place where needed. How did Ronak know that the need for strength would come too soon! Here is the next thing, After the party, Ronak arrived at the hostel. Nilesh had already come into the room And Ronak went straight to bed.
"Oyy, you spoke in the morning, to make the girl a bride. Got someone? " Ronak said.

"You didn't even pay the price on the first day and you became a hero!" Nilesh said.
"I do not know how to live in fear. I have learned to overcome fear and move forward. One of the girls smiled at me. " Ronak said.
"Want to see what it's like? " Nilesh said.
"Oyy, put a smile on her face." Ronak said.
"New girl, who's smiling?" Nilesh said.
"Yours, now I will hear from my mouth." Ronak said.
"So far, so good! I hear you speak Let's move on. Then, I smile too. Let's just say the Love-line is through. " Nilesh said.
"Yes. Then what Talked a bit when I went next to her. We became friends. " Ronak said.
"Happened from your scandal fight student. It's not one, all the girls line you up. What was the name? " Nilesh said.
"Madhavi." Ronak said.
"Madhav's Madhavi." Nilesh said.
"Is there any Madhav?" With surprise Ronak said.
"No,no, It's just joke. Celebrate. Arrange me in her sisterhood after the girl is Loveship. " Nilesh said.
"One hundred percent." Ronak said.

That's when Ronak got the call from that girl. Talks started. This became a fun life.
(Looking to the future) Weeks before the day of the attack.

Ronak was sitting in a corner of the room crying. Was suffocating, don't know what happened to him? He could not stay. The rope hung on the fan. Probably to be hanged.

..

Part 3 (beginning of understanding)

Ronak and Madhavi talk about love every day. If both go to college, both sit together, Sometimes nights would pass in conversations. Assessment writing comes in semester, Writing along with it, And Both had fun. Running away from the hostel to see the movie, Going outside hostel and living a cool life. So one day it happened that Ronak was standing at the back window of the room talking to Madhavi, There was a small noise coming from the room above him. Looks like a lot of people must have gathered there But there was talk of silencing.

"Madhavi, I'll call you later." Ronak said as he hung up the phone.

He immediately climbed up from the back balcony and went into the room. There were four students doing something. He was sketching into civil engineering work. What is the reason for stopping talking?

"What, what movement? Keep working, keep moving forward. " Ronak said.

"Yes, that's right." One said.

Everyone was busy, so Ronak walked out of the front door and into the room without saying a word.

"When I went into the room, These people were drawing the civil engineering plan. The plan-sketch was for hostels and colleges. It is true that he was asked to draw a plan from college, but from that voice it seemed that he could be a little older than me. Maybe five or six years older. The figure was written on the back of the plan, no unit like meter was written. Everything was fine, but most of all, there

was fear and sweat on everyone's face." Ronak said in his mind. That is why Nilesh reached there.
"What do you think, brother?" Nilesh asked.
"One work!" Ronak asked.
"Yes, brother!" Nilesh said.
"Go to civil engineering class, Tell me in the evening what everyone is doing. " Ronak said.
"Information about the girl or something?" Nilesh asked.
"We have to see what works. No girls matter." Ronak said.
"Yes, it doesn't matter." Nilesh said.
Nilesh then resumed his work. In the evening the hostel met Ronak.
"Ronak, everyone was busy. Was the work of a surveyor, So it was going to be a laboratory department plan-sketch for the people, So those student had to go to a hospital outside the college. If the plan-sketch seemed small, these people would still be learning. There were only two girls left,
When he went to talk, she called me alone and slapped me. " Nilesh said.
"Never mind." Ronak said.
"Why didn't you tell me what happened?" Nilesh asked.
"I'll let you know when the time comes." Ronak said.

When all went to dinner in the evening, Ronak went to his room and gave him photos of all the plans, from the smallest spaces in the whole room. Then he went to dine in the hall, Ronak was looking for people in the hall but did not find them. The night was dark, Suddenly five students came in at different times

while Ronak was sitting down to eat, And all five sat in separate places. All five of them were watching Ronak.
Ronak seemed to know nothing And began to have fun in his own tune. Ronak probably talked and had fun with everyone he didn't know, even though he knew something. Ronak thought it would be fun to find all this. He ate and went all the way alone, The five students were then chasing him. Ronak knew so he called Madhavi and tried to change the subject.
"Madhavi, it's night time, having fun." Ronak said.
Listening to him like this, five student Felt that Ronak was not thinking of anything And those five student kept going. The fact is that Ronak did not call Madhavi. Then he went out and hid any place behind them. Finally five student reached the hostel without speaking. Ronak was thinking then. "Five students needed to chase me, That sounds like a big scandal. I have to understand the whole plan. "
(Look to the future)

Ronak was digging in front of a corner wall in the garden a short distance from the dark hostel at night. From there he found a cache of weapons. He took a small gun from it.

...

Part 4 (Confusion)
The next morning Ronak was lying on the bed with everything open and thinking about everything. There came the garbage man and when the boom fell, he widened his eyes and suddenly stood up and thought in his mind, "Something must have been found in the

trash. Something must have been thrown away."
Then, without speaking, Ronak tied his mouth to the back of the road and went to the trash can. And everything was looking for something not found But when garbage man brought the trash from the upstairs room, Ronak asked the brother for the basket. Saying I have lost a piece of paper, Then he saw all the papers but found nothing but a plan. Still took the plan and went to the room. Then Nilesh would ask him what is all this? So Ronak did the whole thing from the beginning to the end.
"So seem to be planning something big? If nothing else, all students are the same." Nilesh said.
"If were a student, why do look over twenty-five? Why are scared, why are chasing me, and why isn't the big thing mixing with anyone?" Ronak said thoughtfully.
"Any wish." Nilesh said.
"Help one last time, it doesn't matter if it's true." Ronak said.
"Yes, what to do?" Nilesh asked.
Then the whole plan is explained to him. According to the plan, by targeting all the money of Nilesh, Ronak climbed up the balcony and hid all the money in his room when no one was in the room. Then he comes back to Nilesh, Ronak was then running very fast on the road ahead And Nilesh was screaming thief. Then all the boys of the hostel ran after him but he had a handkerchief tied around his mouth And the clothes were new so no one could recognize them. Ronak ran away from there and no one saw him. Then Ronak came out of the back bathroom of the hostel from the common bathroom when the clothes

were second. And what happened in front of everyone who spoke?
"Stolen." Nilesh said.
"So where is the thief?" Ronak said.
"Run away." Nilesh said.
" How long has it been?" Ronak asked, in a way he didn't know.
"half an hour." Nilesh said.
"Check the hostel room, get the money from somewhere?" Ronak said.

Then Nilesh obeys and goes to see his way in all his rooms. When the money came out of that room he went to tell everyone that there were five men. When was called to the office, Five student did not know what was going on, so Nilesh went to his room to check and found a pen drive. There is no better plan for Ronak than to carefully check his room. When Ronak inserted the pen drive into his laptop and started looking at everything, the pen drive did not open. Had to be decord, But Ronak knew how to decord because he loved hacking so he learned everything on his own. Decoding found some people's photos and dates.
"Hey, these are photos of one hundred and thirty-one men, fifteen to twenty of whom I saw in college. There are plans to do something on March 26. " Ronak tells Nilesh. Then a plan which saw a quadrangle mark in front of a corner in a rectangle.
"The virus has entered." Ronke said.
"I don't understand?" Nilesh said.
"That is, if this pendrive is inserted in a laptop other than their laptop, it will check the IP address for thirty

seconds and if no address is found, the file will be blown away." Ronak said.

"So you were right." Nilesh said.

"But what if the quadrilateral in that rectangle shows a corner?" Ronak said.

"Brother, I can't think like you. There are two weeks left until March 26th. Are you going to tell the police? " Nilesh asked.

"There is no proof, don't believe the police. He found out that if the matter reached the police, he would do the work before the time he was supposed to do on March 26. Now these people don't need to catch up at all. We have to see what is drawn in the plan and what the plan wants to say. The police will arrest him along with the proof. " Ronak said.

"Ok." Nilesh said.

"The police are right, brother. The check would have been done at our request. At last the stakes are high. " Ronak said.

"Then these people will know if the pen drive is gone?" Won't you work sooner? " Nilesh asked.

"Pendrive has not opened them yet. Because whatever the pen drive is, even once inserted it looks a little worn out, It does not appear. Secondly, I did not see any laptop or computer in his room. If you want to study, you need an Android phone, They had Nokia's small phone. That means they haven't even gotten a laptop yet, Leave the pen drive in the corner of their room. They would feel like he broke down in anger. So he will call and tell the leader, For a hint of something else. Until then, I will check everything from the mark of this quartet. " Ronak said.

"What does a college plan mean?" Nilesh asked.
"There is no trace of it." Coming to the thought, "What is the area of the college? Check it out." Ronak said.
(Look to the future)

Ronak's hand is fractured and he came to someone's house half-dead, Blood is dripping from his head on the bandaged body. In that case, he killed someone with a gun. Who ????????

...

Part 5 (War of Love)

Ronak then began to chase after the creature. He would go to the college terrace and look through binoculars in the garden next to the college. He saw and saw his girlfriend Madhavi hiding behind a bush in the corner of the garden with a boy. Ronak was surprised and ran to the spot. Ronak's brain and heart were so numb that he didn't realize it and went straight to the spot and grabbed them both.
"Madhavi, is this all?" Ronak asked sharply.
"My best friend." Madhavi replied as if nothing had happened.
"I saw everything there." Ronak said.
"Then you keep an eye on me." Madhavi said.
"I was watching, because I was afraid I would lose you." Ronak changed the answer after another.
"Yes, listen. I have a boyfriend, do what you can. I am here, "said Madhavi.
"Then what about my feeling?" Ronak asked in a broken voice.
"My life is my choice, seeing you understand and love." Madhavi said to Ronak in a loud voice.

"I can't live without you. If you had to do this, you should have said it first! I will not move forward. " Ronak said in a broken voice.

"If you do, forget me. I'm someone else's now. And if you can't live without me, die, yes, do a favor, die without writing in a letter because I don't like going to jail. " With so much talking, Madhavi kept going.

It was very difficult to save Ronak now. As he walked away, tears welled up in his eyes and he could barely contain himself. Went to college but didn't pay any attention in class, Nilesh looked at him and thought that something big must have happened but it was not like that. Even if Ronak and Madhavi fall apart, it is difficult to save Ronak, And second, Ronak forgot all about the war he was ready to face in the future. Instead of finishing class, he went straight to the hostel.

(Last paragraph of part 2.)

When Ronak arrived at the hostel, he tied the rope to the fan and did not close the door. Nilesh also used to come back running as he did not come for dinner. The hostel was also far away. Tears welled up in Ronak's eyes. Ronak climbed on the table And the rope tied around Ronak neck, he commit try suicide. And Nilesh came immediately pushed him down on lag.

"What were you doing here?" Nilesh said.

"If Madhavi betrayed me, i committed try suicide." Ronak said.

"So what's the point of dying?" Nilesh said.

"I didn't know what to do." Ronak said.

"Do you realize anything?" Nilesh said.

"Don't say anything right now: go ahead. Shut up for a minute. " Then looking behind the door, No one appeared, meaning, "Yes, now." Ronak said.

"I understand you first and last. Brother you is not waiting to sacrifice himself to save this whole college. If you die for a girl, saving this college will not be difficult, it will be almost impossible. No one can be saved. Today the whole college does not even know and when it is known then you will be the hero of this college and everyone will have hope on you that you will get them out alive. However, I don't think anything will happen. But if you are not, then there is no one. No proof, just an idea is going to go wrong, It's not up to you to put the whole college at stake for one girl. Don't sacrifice college for a girl. " Nilesh said angrily.

"Who said, I'm sacrificing college. I was thinking of everything and working. These people stay behind me all day and these people keep an eye on what I do or are able to do. So I made a plan, I said Madhavi that a boy should do love ship and break up with me. Doing so will make me cry and make my condition worse. I then told Madhavi everything that this was happening in the hostel so she accompanied me, Then, according to the plan, he continued to chase till now. You were also coming back because if you don't come then who will save me? So I came in front of you and sat down sad. You also came behind me and hid behind that door and they felt like their brains were out of place. They will think that there is nothing I can do and I will do everything right now. The whole college has taken the responsibility to save, I will save

most of all. Probably everyone! " Ronak said.
"You're really out of my mind, man." Nilesh said with a smiling face.
(Look to the future)

Ronak was dressed like a common man while running, NSG commandos shot him Which fell off the shoulder.

..

Part 6 (obstacle)
"Brother, don't reach your mind." Nilesh said.
"Now we have to understand that plan. " Ronak said.
"What will be the area of the college?" Nilesh said
*"3 * 1.6 km square." Ronak said.*
"Walking in a jungle-like area behind the campus building for another 500 meters! It's important. You're welcome, I'm not such a daring man." Nilesh said.
"So do you. Otherwise, I will break into the house and kill. " Ronak said.
"Yes, let's go now." Nilesh said. On the way out of the two of them, Ronak and Nilesh came across a large fence and Ronak and Nilesh came across many big stones and some broken thick ones.
"It's annoying. I knew this was going to happen when I came with you." Nilesh said.
"There's still time, if you want to go back, go away!" Ronak said.
"I'm gone." Nilesh said.
"Where did you go, so I can fight with a stranger player but in such a road I got torn." Ronak said.
"If you burst, I will have to be uprooted." Nilesh said.
"I'm just sitting to cut." Ronak said.
After walking about two kilometers, Ronak saw the

snake on the road.

"Ohh, Shiva Shiva Shiva Shiva." Ronak said. The whole thing got wider.

"What happened?"Nilesh said. Nilesh doesn't know situation.

"Nothing to take forward, Debt or not. " Ronak said.

"Why?" Nilesh said.

"Snake is appearing." Ronak said fear voice.

"Oh, what about you now?" When Nilesh found out, he started trembling.

"Don't vibrates body." Ronak said.

"So what do I do?" Nilesh said.

"Let me make a gesture with the body movement, I will start running with the situation and you also." Ronak said.

"I don't know this situation." Nilesh said.

"Run fast." Ronak said.

"Yes, brother." Nilesh said.

"The snake ladder is playing." Ronak said.

"Cut with 99 coming up, We will come up first. " Nilesh said.

"Not at first, Run will go straight to me." Ronak said, Running away.

"Don't run as fast as the dog fell behind, just run at a speed of 360 per minute." Nilesh said.

"Don't run upside down with two speeds!" Ronak said.

"We're going deep, where we're going, where we're going." Nilesh said.

"Yes, that's right. Now, if there was an examination for constable or police inspector, we would come first. Because 1 kilometer of 1 minute, I think, is what we're

running right now. " Ronak said.
"Atleast we got back to the hostel." Nilesh said.
"Basis feet like yours will be inflamed now." Ronak said.
"It happens when there is inflammation, burn means escape." Nilesh said.
"Come on, nothing. You're the only judge I'm not in the mood to come. I will go to bed in the hostel room as I will be on police duty tomorrow. That's it. It's just joke." Ronak said.

Ronak then began to think to himself and night fell. Then he left alone with the light of his mobile on night. How much was in between. Frightened by the sounds of small insects, he was about to cover three kilometers, finally he did not lose courage and kept moving. There was fear in his mind but the life of the hostel was in his hands. When he got out, he got a mobile phone stuck in the road. He hacked his mobile phone by inserting USB cable in his mobile phone. Then he was amazed at what he saw and began to think, "I was right, This firing is to be done directly when the farewell party is in everyone's class on the 26th. Means direct attack, Hostel and college attack, I will do anything to save everyone. " After thinking so much, when the light of the mobile turns on, it feels as if it has been dug before the soil. He starts digging without thinking. Then he gets a big box that he can't lift. As soon as the box opens, He is surprised. Because it had guns, grenades, snipers, machine guns. This was to may be the largest attack to date as the machine gun and sniper had not been used by the terrorist in the attack so far. So he took some guns, took a sniper and a machine gun and buried them a short distance away. He took four small guns with him and went to the hostel with a magazine like fifty. He came to the hostel and told Nilesh about this and showed him the gun.

"For the first time in my life!" Nilesh said with surprise.

"I have to fire." Ronak said.

"What?" Nilesh said in surprise.

..

Part 7 (War)

"Now that proof has been found, let the police know!" Nilesh asked.

"Yes, my uncle's boy is an NSG commando, let me tell him." Ronak said.

Ronak called his brother and told him everything. The officer then told his chief everything.

"How much information is true?" Chief officer said.

"Perfect information, Then where did you want to do it? I wanted to be an army officer, but I wanted to be a graduate. Yes made up any mind to do it first. I want the police and the trust man the college and hostel to be vacated?" Ronak asked.

"Yes, but very hard. If you want, do it first. It is necessary now. Later, if they want to attack, they will get votes. I salute you, brother. If you are looking for a risk. The whole country will be proud of you, Ronak." Chief officer said.

"Ok, Sir. I will do it. First of all save college and you save me. Thank you so much sir." Ronak said.

There were three days left till March 26. Ronak

and Nilesh had breakfast and were returning to the hostel. By then, all the classes in the college were full. Ronak and Nilesh were given a few days off by his brother beacase dead-line(Time limit.). No one was seen on the streets of the college, all were from their own class and all the masters were sitting in their office rooms.

There was a graded blast in the office room for three days. There was a terrorist student in all the class already so he was barred from coming out. This side Ronak and Nilesh were completely surprised.

"Ronak, what happened?" Nilesh said.

"Fear, fear started all student." Ronak said.

"The NSG may have called the police and the trustee and the matter may have got out of there. So terrorist attacked this early. If the college becomes vacant then work is not possible. And the brother told me, the name of the police is Deepak Dave. I will catch him if i win from here. Many will be killed in the blast, and all will have to answer. " Ronak said.

The hostel student was then apprehended by five men as both approached the hostel. Nilesh was scared when Ronak gave a gun to Nilesh as Ronak and Nilesh were walking inside the conference bluetooth in their ears.

"listen me, Rarely does anyone god give such an opportunity.This is an opportunity to show humanity. There is no need to be afraid here, courage is needed. Maybe even if we become martyrs, this country will think that no one can pay for the favors we have taken. The prayers of the parents of all the students

join us. If we don't fight, no one will fight. We all have a chance to save, let's save everyone. Maybe one of us survives and the other survives. Let me tell you a story." Ronak said.

{ Mission Challenge (Ahmedabad Attack.)

Part 7.1 Destruction.

The war was and still is when India became independent. The fight did not stop or will not. The country was liberated on August 15, 1947. But taking an insider, Mohammad Ali Jinnah has already demanded a separate country for Muslims. It demanded the annexation of states like Junagadh of Gujarat, Hyderabad and Kashmir of India etc. to Pakistan. But the people there wanted to live in India. Then Sardar Vallabhbhai Patel himself united the kingdom to live in India. This split led to a major split between Hindus and Muslims, That part was the warning of the greatest battle of all time to come. India had nothing to fear from the Hindus who were Muslims. Pakistan Jamaat was afraid of Muslims. Indian Muslims in India were living together. Here, it is true that if the two stay together, it is true, and at night, at dinner, one day, the story is connected with the mission challenge.

So far many terrorist attacks have been seen on TV, It has been read in the history books but an attack which is not written in any history book or the secret behind it has been hard to find so far.

26 July 2008 Ahmedabad terrorist attack.

The attack was large, but fifty-six people were killed. In Ahmedabad, Bapunagar, Naroda, Nikol, Civil Hospital, Kalupur and many other areas were taken in the bomb blast. This was really annoying for Ahmedabad. For those who live somewhere in Gujarat, Ahmedabad is a city for business, Manchester of India is called cried day-Black day. Blood lines started appearing in Ahmedabad, instead of mud, flesh filled eyes started appearing, if someone's hands got separated from the torso, if someone's head fell off, if someone went to save someone's life, he became a martyr. The most horrific situation was in Bapunagar when the injured were taken to the ambulance and a bomb was planted in the ambulance. If they was taken to a civil hospital from another place, a bomb was placed in the hospital. Does it mean that the attack which took such a horrible form became a shame for Ahmedabad that what is the safest place? Probably a safe place to stay. The whole attack was shown from the first line of the news on TV in people's homes. It seems to everyone that people are dying in front of us. Many people call their loved ones and get the news that no one was injured in the attack. Just this day turned out to be so terrible and the next day one thing came to everyone's face "Fear". What the terrorists wanted was made possible. It was a situation that no one expected. Someone's boys were sitting in the tuition class all night hungry and thirsty and even their family members could not reach. So they came back home after seeing a bomb blast in front of someone. Ahmedabad was on fire on this day.

I have come up with a story on this attack. In a society in Naroda area, there are two twin houses, one house was occupied by a Hindu family

and the other by a Muslim family. It has a son and daughter in a Muslim family with his mother and father and a son in a Hindu family with his mother and father.
(Hindu family: son's name is Mitesh, his father's name is Piyush and his mother's name is Ashaben,
Muslim family: son's name is Ehsan, daughter's name in Nazi, and in it mommy daddy's name is Reshma and Iqbal.)
The family lived happily ever after, Lived happily but had to play bloody Holi this day.
[Writer Hemilkumar P Patel : This story is not written in anyone's life family. Just showing how important an empty family is. Thank you.

..

Part 7.2 The beginning of the story, the challenge of the mission
26 July 2019

Eleven years later, there is a house in a rural area of Ahmedabad. Twenty to twenty-five blacksmiths have fallen into it. Many try body movement. Shaking the bones, they straighten the body and look at each other. Many people shoot each other in the middle of the night. And surprisingly, all are Army officers. There is no outsider. Some people are killed and those who are alive are killing each other, Such an atmosphere has arisen. It is unknown at this time what he will do after leaving the post. Is it a sudden attack or a deliberate decision? It is a very unknown thing. Let's skip this.
26 July 2008 Ahmedabad Attack.
Time: 4 p.m.

Both family members are sitting in the yard, The sons and daughters are seventeen and eighteen years old, This is young. Yet They spends time talking and playing something. Right now cricket is being played and talking is happening.

Mitesh said. "Brother, you both cut my beting."

Ehsan said. "Don't said, mine, my bet after my sister."

Nazi said. "Don't play game, even if I didn't want to play, you forcibly brought me."

Soon after, Mitesh's father Piyush came and said. "Ehsan, if you call your father, we talked yesterday about going shopping and going out all day.

Nazi said. "Yes, My family is ready, mother and Asha aunty are both standing outside the gate of the society. We have not forgotten by preparing."

Mitesh said. "Yes, let's not be late."

Iqbal came out and said. "Yes, let's get ready. Let's get rid of it all. "

Mitesh said. "The Nazi are angry today."

Iqbal said. " She had a headache. Gave the medicine, now let's go. "

Both the families look very happy and both the families did not differentiate between God and Allah. Going to both temples and mosques. Now the time has come. These people were the first to reach Bapunagar Haveli. They also went inside to see the structure of the mansion, it was the temple that many people used to come to see. Piyush parked his car in the mall in front of the mansion. The two families then moved to the mansion. Piyush forgot the mobile and sent it to Mitesh to pick it up. Mitesh went to pick up the phone.

Don't know what will happen to Janaki Nath (God name.) tomorrow, but Mitesh was only man, All were the humun culture. This is the time created by God, Do not know what sins were punished at this time. Mitesh take the phone from the car, Lock the car and leaves for the mansion, Soon the first bomb blast in the mansion took place. Bapunagar had already been taken. Mitesh was out alone, His eyes became red. He still doesn't know what's going on. Understanding that a nightmare is going on in front of me but the reality has to be human. Mitesh Heart's family is not crying because they are watching the mansion from a distance. Far away on the left side of Mitesh is a vegetable truck, All standing and watching, The bomber struck shortly after noon in front of a car packed with explosives. Bomb blast dropped a few particles of the bomb and started bleeding from his hand. He shakes his hand and pulls out the thing that hit him. So that thing turned out to be an iron spear. I mean, it wasn't an RDX bomb, but a steel pressure bomb made by an electrician. Looking around, one man put a bag on his bicycle and ran away. So Mitesh started chasing him. An eighteen-year-old boy decided to take up the fight. The bicycle exploded as he drove away. As he walked along, there was an alley beside him where two men were talking.

One said. "All survived."

Another said. "Yes, sir. We're a little late. "

One said. "Blast had to be done sooner." Hearing all this, Mitesh goes to that line.

Mitesh said angrily. "Both of you are happy. Enjoyed seeing all this? "
Another man said. "Who are you, brother? Do you know who to talk to?" The first man there stops him, And refuses to speak in gestures.
Mitesh said. "Just five minutes ago, my whole family was devastated by the blast of the mansion. All died. No one can move around peacefully because of people like you. Don't want to overdo it. I remember the faces of both of you. Now, My name is Mitesh, in the next ten years, I will come to you with all kinds of training and face to face revenge. No one will be killed later and I will kill all those who are behind this. Today is my mission and today is my challenge. I am challenging this mission in front of you. I have time with you, I am alone, now you can kill me, but when i come after ten years, don't even give you a chance. I will kill both of you and your all member. "
One said. "No, no. I will not kill you now. The pleasure of beating you will come only after ten years. Your challenge is accepted. "

....

Part 7.3 (Preparation)

Mitesh said so much and left, The terrorist did not say anything. At that time there were seven blasts in Bapunagar and beyond. Now this dark day became known for Ahmedabad. Mitesh would stay home and watch the news and check if his mom and dad had met. With this, Mitesh's days began to pass. Then when the 26/11 attacks happened, Mitesh kept checking everything at a young age.

This little boy at the age of eighteen does not

realize any worldliness and he reached Mumbai at such a time. Mitesh saw him in front of my eyes even today. Looking around, Mitesh went to the place where the attack took place and started investigating. Don't tell anyone, And there was news that all these came across the sea, So he took the boat himself and went out on the way. And in a few months, the way the terrorists came here, Mitesh got there under the name of Altaf. Speaking of which, if the family needed it, he reached out by showing the wrong ID. There he started working on a tea kettle and decided who was the gang that did all this. So he found a gang whose name was known as Ismailbhai. So this direct kept going to the area of Ismailbhai who was a little boy. After going there, he talked to all of them and finally reached Ismail.

"From meeting outside, The more you go, the better! " Mitesh (Altaf) said.

"You want to do something!" Ismail said.

"I sold tea all my life, I worked in a hotel. Now I want to do it for the sake of paradise. " Mitesh (Altaf) said.

"Where do you know, about us?" Ismail said.

"I know the 26/11 date." Mitesh (Altaf) said.

"So you are perfect, Allah or you want paradise pages in the court. " Ismail said.

That's how I joined him, two years later. Ismail trained in our base. He was finally prepared for the attack after three years of training. This time the whole of Gujarat was made a victim. So he decided that now is the time to come back to Gujarat. He was to return from Karachi port to Kandla port. So before this, the police took Mitesh to Kandla port. And

Mitesh killed everyone who came in the boat. And when Mitesh dropped the time bomb in ismail base, he blew up the whole gang. Mitesh reached Gujarat in India. He was then taken to court and then told in court that there was a problem with the police arrest. "Yes, there was a problem, Judge Sir. I was there in Ahmedabad five years ago when the terrorists were found after the attack. If something is happening, don't do it until you find it. I know there is a scandal waiting to happen? No need to give proof to the police! No, I stumbled upon what I had. My brother is also a Muslim sir, These people kill Hindus in the name of Muslims. What does a little boy realize? If he is incited against Hindu from birth then he does not know the language of love. If you want to understand, don't believe. Then the whole base of terrorist was settled. These people are provoked by calling Hindu Muslim in Muslim and for me Hindu Muslim is no different, Just in front of me is an India in which Hindus, Muslims, Sikhs or anyone living on this earth are all Indians. And if you punish me for doing so, I want to tell the public. That it spreads terrorist terror, Innocent people to take action after death! Or do you know that taking action is the only way to do this? If I am right, let me make another sacrifice for Mother India. " Mitesh said angrily. The decision was made in favor of Mitesh and he was made a raw agent.

………………..

Part 4 (Invitation)

When Mitesh was called to the Raw office in Delhi, he was scheduled for Gujarat. He was welcomed and called to speak.

That Mitesh explained to everyone, 'I am Mitesh. My childhood was spent at home. Even at the age of understanding, my house kept moving away from me because all dead. There was only one house for me to live in. May spent days in such a state. Then that November when the Taj was attacked I managed to infiltrate Pakistan. Next work you all know everything else. People may think that many family members like me have died there. How many have been orphaned, How many would have been without child, A man earning a living would have been martyred there, How many innocents would have died. Now the thing is that so far only one thing has come and stuck in my mind. It is said that after a crime is committed, I would like to know before the crime that this is going to happen. This can prove raw, Because they have been given that training. With such training, RAW officers go to another country and catch the criminals by running their brains. All these things appear in the movie, but the real thing is, this is not difficult to do, it is impossible. Today I have come to make the impossible to possible. I trained there and Terror base taught me to kill the traitors there. I say there is no traitor for the innocent people of Pakistan. Those who run ISI, attack Sikhs and incite about India are killing the people. Now one thing, listen carefully. That's the thing, "Why are innocent people being killed?" Because the army commander here, the raw officer, the police or whoever is serving the country does not have the strength to kill him. So this frightens the people by killing them. There should be no such fear within the people. People who kill people like us are terrified, That's because standing like us, let's tear it apart. Defending and being martyred while defending has been the most proud thing for the country. I will talk no more. We are very much selected for this job, So let's never let the name of India sink. Jai Hind.'

That's why there is a roar of applause. As he was descending from the stage, what happened now, a man was standing by the door with a towel tied to his mouth. He sees Mitesh. Mitesh tried to see the man's mouth as he approached the door, but could not. Then suddenly he starts running, So Mitesh chases. Delhi i.e. Mitesh's first job on Indian soil was to catch this unknown man. Mitesh ran after the man, he was running very fast. Mitesh approached her and pulled towel out of his mouth. However, Mitesh could not see his mouth being on the front side. At last the man who had fallen down took the car and fled. Mitesh also took a car and ran away. After a long chase, his men came to help him. He had a minor accident with Mitesh which hit him a little bit. He was brought to the hospital where Lalit, the commander-in-chief of RAW, arrived.

"It's too much, isn't it?" Lalit said.

"Not at all, because he had a minor accident on purpose." Mitesh said.

"Somehow it was decided that this would be a small thing?" Lalit said.

"When I ran away, after ten to fifteen seconds all the officers came after me. It was such a time duration. Now it is said that seven different men in different vehicles came to his rescue who also had guns. None of this with me. He could kill me if he wanted to,

Don't hit me, Also shot at car tires. Although I was in the middle of it all, he ran away without hitting me. " Mitesh said.
"Why would he want to be saved?" Lalit said.
"Maybe giving me a message, Terrorists will be watching over us. The message may be that I have ruined his whole work here, So let me see if it spoils our work. Will want to give a net challenge or save the country now. I love the challenge. The biggest mistake was not to kill me. " Mitesh said.

………………..

Part 7.5 War

Lalit kept going from there and then Mitesh called someone and then said, "Yeah, It will be fun to move on. However, if you had kept the speed of the vehicle a little lower, you would have been caught. It doesn't matter, be careful. " Mitesh was thinking in his mind after putting down the phone. "Now, In India, it would seem that if all the work I have done is to be answered by terrorists, then the whole force will be on the lookout for them. Then no terrorist takes the risk. I have to go upside down. Because this accident has made people think that it must have been carried out by a terrorist. However, I have paid for the accident. Now find out who caused the accident. I will uproot the terrorist organization, grow the organization."

Mitesh was happy when the news started coming in the news. And the terrorist who initially met and challenged him during the bomb blast was sitting at home in Kolkata, They two man was happy to see the news. Then this side went to Delhi for a few days and Mitesh got the same and he came back to

the office.
"Did anyone know who the man was?" Lalit said.
"Yes, the man I challenged when the blast took place in Ahmedabad." Mitesh said. "What's in a name?" Lalit said.
"Mohammed Mustafa." Mitesh said.
"Any information about that?" Lalit said.
"The name left is a ghost. Because it disappears like a ghost. I'll find out though. Give me permission to go to Kolkata. " Mitesh said.
"Why do you want to go to Kolkata?" Lalit said.
"My mission, my work, I know everything alone." Mitesh said.
"Okay, let's go. I'll save everything here. Don't have an accident again. " Lalit said.
"No, believe me." Mitesh said.

From there Mitesh kept going. Mitesh came home to get clothes prepared for Kolkata. It so happened that all the peppers in his neighborhood were missing in the blast, However, he has removed the garland from the photos of Ehsaan and Nazi. Now remove the garland, did he/she die in the blast, then why he is alive? When Mitesh left for Kolkata, everyone was thinking about what had happened that day. Challenged Mustafa, When Mitesh came back to the side of the mansion, his two brothers and sisters were standing outside crying. Mitesh was surprised to see that, If those people were inside, why did they come out? It so happened that Ehsan had to go to the washroom to see everything in the mansion, so he came out. If Ehsan's phone was with his father, he gave it to Nazi and asked her to give it to Ehsan. So she came out and they both survived. '

Arrived in Kolkata at eight o'clock straight to Mustafa's house, And Mustafa hugged Mitesh. Any way? Enemies of life are being embraced today. Why is this? What happened was that Mitesh threatened to kill Mustafa in the future, So are you getting a hug now? Something like this happened. (Remember, the last paragraph will be found in Part 2.)

....

Part 7.6 Challenge

The fact was something else. It is happen that when Mitesh went to Pakistan, he saw a photo of Mustafa in Ismail's lab. And Mustafa worked at IB (Intelligent buro), Was working for the country. There was a blast that day and Mitesh called his surviving siblings and asked them to find Mustafa. When he was found, he was told that on the day of the attack, Mustafa had said, "Survived." This meant that the terrorist survived, This led to an early attack. Then these two got together and now another plan was being made.

"What's the plan now?" Mustafa said.

"It's time to end the mission. We're being searched." Mitesh said.

"So what now?" Said Ehsan.

"I will next work on the land of Ahmedabad. You did a favor. Take my photo and write on the site of Raw office that I am going to Ahmedabad, my home. There was also a video of made Mustafa leaving the office planning to have an accident to kill me. This

means that those with a raw office will understand that they must have gone somewhere in Ahmedabad to find Mustafa. Giving Mustafa name only, not giving photo.

Everything else I will save. Get out of Ahmedabad in all different vehicles. The terrorist hacking king is coming to India. Another thing was coming to Kolkata, so I changed three vehicles, so I would not have survived, I would have died, "said Mitesh leaving Kolkata.

These people left for Ahmedabad, And the terrorist who had already come to his house there was the terrorist face listening to Lalit Raw's officer. His name was not Lalit: Hanif was from Karachi. Seeing that everyone was sitting at home, Mitesh started talking.

"Ohh Hanif brother." Mitesh said.

"You knew I was Hanif!" Hanif said.

"All I knew was that there was a traitor in the Row office who was delivering the whole plan to Ismail. I knew the name, not the face, so I planned an accident. Jaya Mustafa was running ahead of me. My brother Ehsan was behind you, So instead of taking a car and coming to my rescue, you went to a place with some extra security when everyone was a terrorist. You went there so Ehsan also came after you And your whole office has seen Ehsan. Then did you check who might have tried to hit me, Ehsa was spotted by sleeper cell men from different places holding a conference in that video calling And his video was sent to NSG, RAW, IB, DRDO everywhere. By now those people must have been caught and you

came to Ahmedabad to kill me at my request. You don't know when Mustafa was out of name, you were looking for me instead of him? Your mistake. " Mitesh said.

"If a mistake is made, let's correct it!" Hanif said in surprise.

Then the firing and fighting started. A lot of people were beaten here, just these four men were fighting. Mustafa was martyred here and killed Hanif.

(Mission over.)

This strength came in many works of Mitesh. The countrymen's voice is proud of RAW, IB and many hidden country agencies.

....

(Present.)

"In the same way, sometimes we have to go to the battlefield." Ronak said.

Nilesh got a hug with tears in his eyes. Ronak cried for the first time that day, as he and Nilesh both believed in each other more than their brother. We will live or we will meet death, Save of this college and hostel was with both of them. People who have been blasted cannot be saved, But those who survived could be sent home safely. The duo stormed into the hostel from behind with tears in their eyes. Put a silencer in the gun. Ronak decided to kill three and Nilesh two. One by one, opened the door of the room and killed him immediately. All the students of the hostel started looking in front of him.

....

Part 8 (War)

Killing five terrorists in the hostel, Nilesh and

Ronak were all standing there.
"Listen to me, brothers. The help of a hostel should be sought first when you have to do any function in college, The hostel student should be spoken to when decorating the college, Hostel if students are outside and they need some help. We don't know how much we are helping college in this way. Something different this time, This time it is a game of giving life, brothers. These people are not going to leave us, These people are going to kill one by one. This has hijacked the college. (Middle story season 2) Don't know what is necessary but these people are in the mood to kill. Will kill me too.

I just want to say that hostel students never no say in any work, This saying should be kept true. Student's father/mother any member who pray on our lives must be saved. At present, the parents of all the students of the college are sad. Can't you put good hope in those people's mouths! We've been helping people from college and all campuses, So can't help this time! Hostel Attack This world would also call a hostel student attack. that the hostel was not attacked, The hostel's student attack on terrorist. Wouldn't you feel better if the world said that? "Ronak said hopefully.
"We all join you, don't attack the hostel: the hostel will attack." Said one student.

With that said, all the students in the entire hostel are told to take whatever weapon the gun is graded.
"Listen to me now. Time is short, All that is to be done is that the college building is seven hundred

meters away from the hostel. Every gun needs a silencer. Just join me. Now, every ten minutes, there should be half a team to separate and destroy the building terror team. Then three or four men voluntarily turned their faces in the opposite direction and fell to the ground. Because no terrorist should come in from outside. Strength man will go inside. The one whose body is small will lie on one side or the other on all four sides of the building and keep an eye on it. Now I talked to my brother and got the news that it will be four or five hours after he gets permission and you have to save here for another five hours i.e. ten hours. Now, if you take a magazine like Wish Twenty-Five of the gun you have taken, nothing will fall. No police will come now to carry out the attack as per situation as I have told my brother to stop the police from coming in because if he comes in there will be more attacks. Now the thing is that those people should not see us from the building, when it is near the window or door, you should take space and hide, Not to become Sultan Mirza. Got it, let's go to college and attack you all now. This time it was not a hostel attack but a hostel students attack in history. Thank you. "Ronak said.

Now this side of the college were all hiding in their respective places and killing whatever appeared. Ronak felt that nobody's name, Ronak also looked like 26/11 this time And were immediately killed. All the students were trying to hide in different places. If there was a lone student somewhere, if he was going to kill a terrorist, these people would kill him mercilessly too.

According to Ronak, everyone went to the college side. Ronak took the M-4 and NT-242 sniper. So looking through his binoculars he saw a man in the window then he sat there and shot him from a distance. When this happened, the terrorists were afraid to come out of the window.

"Now, no commando has come, who is this?" Asked each other terrorist.

"The way he was shot, the way he was hit with a big gun is mine. The commando has missed this. First let go of the college people. Let the lessons keep an eye on the key outside. "The boss said.

When this happened, everyone started looking outside. Now why did Ronak shoot, Because the way Ronak wanted everyone to be different and get around the building, he reached out to the students of the hostel. All hid around the wall of the college building, a thick twig lying on itself, so that no one would suspect that anyone was here!

....

Part 9 (Fight of Hardcore)

Nilesh was hiding under the wall of the college And Ronak was firing from the east side of the college behind a thicket three hundred meters away if anyone looked out the window.

"Everyone reached their position, Nilesh?" Ronak asked.

"Yeah Ronak. No one coming out of a window upstairs?" Nilesh asked.

"No one appears right now. I go to the south side of the college, there are three workshops. There are no students. That would be Safe Zone. Hiding four or

five people above the workshop, Let's adjust the position and go inside. Because if all there is found to be hidden, then it is over. Now I'll run, maybe someone will come out to kill someone, Don't let the terrorist do whatever he wants. I'm leaving now my current position, "Ronak said.

While Ronak was running away, Nilesh was hiding in the thicket. He saw Ronak running away. And was giving cover. Suddenly, a terrorist appeared, but Ronak was fleeing when a bullet struck him in the shoulder. Screaming softly, he hid behind a thicket. Ronak saw on the shoulder and the wound was not too big. Ronak was hit in the shoulder by a bullet that hurt him even more. He had seen Nilesh when the bullet hit him and he was scared.

"Ronak Ronak, brother!" Nilesh Asked in surprise.

"Yes, yes the eyes are open." Ronak said.

"We picked up the gun at the behest of I doesn't even know how to fire." Nilesh said.

"Do you have a gun?" Ronak said.

"M4" Nilesh said.

"Is there scope?" Ronak said.

"Yes." Nilesh said.

"Then get ready to shoot. Remember the load on the shoulder will be heavy, Shoot the body tightly."said Ronak.

"Yeah but who's kill?" Nilesh asked.

"Do you see everything south and west of the college in the back side?" Ronak asked.

"Yes." Nilesh said.

"Come on, you're in position. Go to sleep down first. I felt as if the bullet had gone from bottom to top,

That's the shooter, Sleep on place. He does not know our plan. (Nilesh does as Ronak speaks.) The way you look south and west. Now increase the zooming of your scope and rotate between the workshop and the college space, if any movement appears. " Ronak said.

"Yes, one appears." Nilesh said.

"Now listen, if there is movement, his gun will be in this direction. Can you see his gun? " Ronak said.

"Can't see the gun, he is going between the thick, Just his left shoulder and legs are visible all over the outside. " Nilesh said.

"Yes, listen to me. When you shoot at the left shoulder, it will be pulled to the left, And as soon as his little head appeared, you shot another shot in the head. Can you do that? " Ronak said.

"You I do that. We are not alone. We are together." Nilesh said.

Then, as Ronak had said, when the first shot was fired at the shoulder, his head was pulled to the left and he immediately finished the second shot.

"Ronak, It's done." Nilesh said.

"Yes, that's right. Now I'm leaving the sniper. I also have M4, I will keep hitting whatever appears as it comes out. You have informed everyone that even if they are asleep, they should be standing in all the windows as if they are standing. The other thing is to be ready to shoot and kill as soon as terrorist arrives. Remember to be prepared to run if you get graded, I'm on run the workshop side, So I'll cover up what I see, "said Ronak.

Somewhere there was a shooting. On the south side,

his voice came to Ronak.
"Hey Ronak, the south side looks any problem." Nilesh said.
"Who's on the south side?" Ronak said.
"Rohit may think so. Can't save alone." Nilesh said.
"Do one thing, If you come back upside down and hit someone in the window, keep hitting. I am going to give cover to Rohit, "said Ronak.
"Yes, it does not matter. Ronak is all the best for this fight, "said Nilesh.
"Yeah, let's name it. Three two one now." Ronak said.

At Ronak's request, Nilesh was sleeping on the outside. If anyone appeared, they would shoot immediately. The fight is terrible shape. Rohit was fighting alone. The college students had to find out where they were hiding. Ronak went to save Rohit, But from the south, it seemed that the terrorists were in large gang numbers. The plan was not to release anyone.

The other thing was that Ronak took all the weapons, So where did the weapons come from? Someone inside was helping him and the fight was getting tougher.

....

Part 10 (Fighting)

"Can you talk to Rohit?" Ronak said.
"No Ronak." Nilesh said.
"As soon as I run there, all can come out and start firing." Ronak said.
"Yes we are ready." Nilesh said. "All the best. I'm running right now." Ronak said.

The shooting continued with Ronak run. Terrorists from the window, Ronak was seen running east to south. Others who later came terrorists, Such as the college building side from the south, All was secretly shooting at everyone. The terrorists were coming to the window to kill Ronak. So the hostel student started firing immediately if he saw any movement from below. The terrorists were shooting at the student and the students at the terrorist. Hostel students see fighting for the first time, Do or die situation, In that state, everyone was suffocating.

There Ronak sat confidently, That Rohit alone will not reach, Ronak has to go there, Ronak was already alone with the team with Nilesh. Now that the terrorists from the south are coming to the college, Ronak goes south from college to cover Rohit, Nilesh and all the others are looking out of the college window from anywhere on the four floors, So all was start firing. If 30 bullets come in one magazine, this will not work, So emptying the magazine, Now it would reload him a while to get another magazine. There is no planning to load one and shoot another.

Nilesh's team south from college, Workshop south from there, Rohit south from there, And finally terrorist. With Nilesh and the other pair, the goods are gone. But no one appeared in the window, he stopped firing after thinking for a while, These people were shooting while sleeping upside down. So what happened is that the terrorist dropped the graded bomb lightly, Seeing that, Nilesh and everyone tried to run away. But when the bomb exploded, these people were far away from the bomb, But explode voice made all student ears tingle. Started screaming inside. Seeing the black smoke all erupted. So now Ronak was surprised, And he was running around thinking that if something happened to someone, it wouldn't happen! So if someone was going to appear from the window, Ronak would run with a small gun and shoot the inverted side. He turned his shotgun on himself when apprehended by a police officer on the porch of the house where the shootings took place. Now shooting him told Nilesh that, 'I give cover, Take everyone to the fifth floor of the workshop, There is a laboratory of the medical department. Go there. '

'Yeah I'm going there, taking everyone.' Nilesh said.

Nilesh did exactly what Ronak wanted. Firstly three workshops while getting there early. Everyone went inside in a safe way. Nilesh said in his mind, "This is a big torture. Terrorists will not die until, Until then, all have to keep escaping. '

Ronak escaped and reached the place where Rohit was. Going there, Ronak saw that Rohit had bled to death. His mouth was unrecognizable, Was stabbed by a bullet. He said to Nilesh, 'Nilesh, Rohit!'

'What happened to Rohit!' Nilesh said.

'Dead.' Ronak said.

Ronak hid behind Rohit's body and came behind tree which had a workshop building next to it. (Ronak's position, South-west first And the space between the second workshop. Ronak sees all three directions, south-east-west, But the north direction is not visible. Alone in the middle of the wall.)

Nilesh felt very tired, Ronak's eyes also turned red. Ronak got angry and went out to shoot. So terrorist hid back due to indiscriminate firing from the front. The sound of the bullet made Ronak feel a little fragile And became very angry And was screaming loudly. Both endurance and empathy were needed. Nilesh from the south side window of the workshop while screaming, And some of his brothers-student went down to look out the window, So there was firing. So Nilesh and his brothers-student started firing south from there. So this is not an uncontrollable fight, Then the sound of bullets started ringing in their ears, Everyone started running out of stamina. All began to cry out loud in their place. This sound was heard by Ronak. Ronak didn't even know what to do then. Fighting alone was taking a terrible form. The college boy who fought to save the innocent, Those people just lost themselves.

This battle was going to take an even more monstrous form. Because the man inside was the one terrorist had met.

……………………..

Part 11 (Destruction.)

Police vans came, many such cops. With the arrival, the first gate of the college was locked. The news channel arrives and immediately starts shooting. (Eight hours left for NSG commandos to arrive.)

So the students of this side hostel did not see any hope. Ronak himself started crying.

"Brothers, it's time to say goodbye. Talk to your family. The call has come from God. " Ronak said in a disappointed voice.

All call home, All talking and crying, The screams were falling. Families who have come out of college, Those whose sons or daughters are trapped inside cannot save themselves. The whole atmosphere was gloomy. The sound of terrorist bullets was heard in all ears. When a police inspector from outside tells Ronak's brother, his brother was also very angry in Delhi. He also started crying, No one had an answer as to what would happen next. The sight became really painful. All were hiding but surrounded on both sides. There was no way out.

But a ray of hope caught Ronak's eye. Ronak was leaning against the east wall, Which made him see everything in the west. There was a hostel boy, heavy body, running in hiding, That way no one can see. But Ronak saw this while running. Ronak had a mild peace of mind. Ronak call him. His name is Roshan.

"Yes, Ronak." Roshan said.

"Take a gun according to your body." Ronak said.

"Where to take position?" Roshan said.

"Wherever you go, There are three tamarind bushes about 200 meters straight. Between the second and the third there will be a little scratched look. There's a machine gun, 150 magazine. " Ronak said.

"Yes, ok. Found gun, wow brother wow. Set it according to my body. " Roshan said.

"Now listen, you're behind them. How many terrorists do you see?" Ronak said.

"Twenty. " Roshan said.

"Now listen, Magazine has to finish the pill, if nothing works inside. That's all there is to it. Now all

eyes will be on me when I go out and shoot a little. At the same time I should see rags. Another thing is to shoot from the waist up, Because I'm also in front of you and it's a machine gun, The bullet will come this far. I'll be sitting down and it will come out of me. " Ronak said.
"One hundred percent will come." Roshan said.

Nilesh and everyone knew that Roshan had reached behind. Then Ronak and a few others came out and started firing in such a way that only the voice could be heard away from the place where Roshan was.

Then the terrorists went out for a while, That is, terrorists attention went to the opposite of Roshan. Immediately after that Roshan came out from behind, Pressing the trigger of the machine gun, The thunder started. Some bullets were also fired from Ronak's head, So he fell asleep holding his head, Said in mind, 'Will pick me up. ' There the rags of the terrorist appeared to Ronak. Roshan turned his gun and killed everyone. The students of the hostel were happy. There Nilesh said in joy and happiness, 'Winner Winner Chicken Dinner. Pubji player won one map. '

The happiness of the boys of the hostel was not surpassed, they became very happy. Tears welled up in my eyes, and I was filled with joy. Roshan and Ronak ran towards him and hugged him. Ronak burst into tears of joy and happiness. On top of this entire he saw a police drone filling up. The police and the media were watching. The whole of India was watching all this. There the inspector knew Ronak,

then called and Ronak got up.
"Well done Ronak." Inspector said.
"Thank you." Ronak said.
"Right now your prowess is being watched live by IB, CBI, RAW, NSG, ARMY. This is a ray of hope. And we all and all commandos, And the whole of India salutes you all at once. " He shouted loudly, 'Jai Hind.' Inspector said.
There this side salutes all the answers from the hostel.
"Sir, now keep one thing in mind. Your eyes will be on us, The media should not be noticed Because if it shows live, our position will fall out. We are still only ten percent settled. There are so many inside. One hundred and thirty-three terrorists, according to the way I discovered, have been killed and now only forty-two. One of the students in our hostel named Rohit who fought till his last breath has been martyred. " Ronak said angrily voice.
"He will be brought out with dignity. It will be as you said," police said with regret.
"Secondly, don't even call me and don't send your men inside. Wait for the NSG. Maybe by then we'll be out. You just keep an eye on us, with this drone. Not live. I'm going to hang up now. Tell me if there's anything. " Ronak said.
"Ronak, the whole country is thankful to you. Good luck." Inspector said.
"I will give my life but now I will not let anyone's life go." Ronak said. So the phone rang. Roshan and Ronak were talking.
"Roshan, even though the whole country thanks us all, If it weren't for you, everything would be over

today. I thank you and I give you the responsibility of this whole work and survival because I fell raw. " Ronak said.

"Brother, the responsibility is yours. If we had not been awakened, we would have stayed in the hostel like Rohit. Now don't talk, let's finish everything,P romise me Ronak, Drink coffee together after battle." Roshan said.

"Promise, not a single terrorist will survive." Ronke said angrily.

....

Part 12 (Step 3)

(Phase III of the battle. Seven hours left for NSG commandos to arrive.)

The drones and the police kept an eye on Ronak all the time. Ronak reached the fifth floor where Nilesh and all were standing. There were only students kept in the south. Finally waiting for Ronak's gesture to come. Ronak arrives with Nilesh.

"Brothers, now the victory is one step. But the big fight is not over yet. I am responsible for all of you. You all must look behind me. So remember I am standing in front of you as a wall. It's time to dump his and move on. This is a fight that involves murder, We will not be punished but we will be rewarded. Now it remains to be seen whether we will stand up or be with God when it comes to receiving rewards. The only thing to keep in mind is to kill directly if you see a terrorist. Don't wait for my gesture there.

Now understand my whole plan. This is a five-story workshop. A four-story college building after a space between eight feet. Now in the college building, in each department, there is a space between the class and the space in a circle. So I want people in every corner of the space to target terrorists so that we can get down. First of all Roshan and I are going to make a big leap from here to there, Then Nilesh, you should stand at the window in the fourth floor to give us cover, Close the window and look through the glass. Someone came out of the front window and shot at us to take him straight from earth to hell. After Roshan and I left, there are four circles in the building, so sixteen brothers will jump. The second time Nilesh you will come. Then someone else will be watching from the window. Got it ???? "Ronak said explaining the whole plan.

"Yes, it doesn't matter." All said in reply.

Ronak and Roshan hid a small gun in different places on their bodies, And the M4 hung a large gun on the shoulder. It will be about the same time Ronak holding a small gun in his hand and reloading. So if a man is seen jumping, he can shoot immediately. When Ronak started running, Nilesh got ready to kill terrorist. Roshan was also preparing.

As Ronak began to run, as he looked out the window, a man appeared with a gun, And when Ronak jumped into the air, Immediately shot into the air position, When he hit his leg, his head hit the window and Nilesh shot him in the head. When Ronak fell on the college building, Roshan ran away. Ronak got up and immediately ran up the stairs. Mouth tied clothes. The police inspector was happy to see such a deed. And said, 'Maybe even if we were inside, we wouldn't be able to do that. Proud of the bravery of the student of Ronak Ans Hostel student. If such people are everywhere then not only the police but also the army people will be at home.'

Different students were arranged on the four sides of the first circle. Nilesh reached here. Knowing that there were three ladders in the same circle, three different ladders i.e. Ronak Roshan and Nilesh arrived.

"Listen, you two have a lot of confidence in yourself, stumbling with appearances. All four of you can't wait for us to land, just shoot to see." Ronke said.

There, men appeared below the circle, and all four began to shoot, hiding there. Shot straight into the head when one foot and down name without giving any chance. Two shots for one man. Ronak's plan was not to waste too many bullets. Ronak Roshan and Nilesh took a small ten-bullet magazine gun and went downstairs at Ronak's signal. Looking up and down the stairs carefully. These three reached the fourth floor i.e. the highest floor. When the men descended the three stairs, no one saw him. All three were moving in different directions looking at the class.

Ronak saw first class, no one appeared, The second class saw three of its terrorists eating food. Ronak gestured to the circle without making a sound. (Remembering that Ronak's right shoulder was bloody,

The shot was fired at the beginning which is given in part 9. And another thing to remember is that Ronak had silencers in all the guns, So terrorist was living in this room, terrorist didn't hear any gunshots.)

Ronak gestured that the three were in class, So he gestured to the class and told them to kill me if they saw anyone coming out. Ronak's eyes went to the graded bomb hanging from his waist. So Ronak gestured how many people came? So the answer from the front is twenty-one.

Everyone was getting cover. So Ronak shot at the graded waist without thinking of anything else. Soon the bomb exploded and Ronak broke into the first classroom so he was not harmed. Now at the sound of these bombs all the terrorists were in the same class as the circle before they left. Now it was dark in and around the classroom where the bomb had exploded. When the terrorist saw the shadow of Ronak and Roshan, he went out and started killing all those above the circle. If he got out of this circle, terrorist would have died. The circle became a whole clean. The bodies of the students were found there while he was watching the second class. Ronak was surprised. The body started sweating. When Roshan and Nilesh also came down, they were amazed to see all this.

"These terrorist are not here to hijack the college, they are here to kill anyone who appears." Ronak's eyes turned red and he said.

Almost all of them found the corpse of a student seventy. A sadness returned. Ronak motioned for the drone to come down from the circle. The police saw all this and sighed. And with that in mind the battle is no longer to win but to give a big answer. Ronak sat down there. At that time its mouth was on the east side and Back on the west side, He then told the men at the top of the circle to come down. Then the other four, jumped over the workshop and reached here and the position changed.

(Complete the third step.)

....

Part 13 (Step 4)

If Roshan was calling from his place with a slight gesture, Ronak's eye went there. These student came down to see everything. Arranging two in each floor, three stood in the opposite direction and three descended. It is to be remembered here that the three are Ronak Roshan and Nilesh, Ronak did not want to risk anyone else's life.

So Ronak suddenly remembered that Madhavi had come to college. Ronak said in his mind, "Where will Madhavi be? I will find out."

When Ronak reached the bottom, four people were arranged on the terrace above the second circle. Ronak stepped forward with an M4 gun in his hand, watching the class. So first the second class had a lock on the front door.

"Locked up, All the terrorists must have returned to the open class. The door will be locked from the outside. No terrorist can think that there is anyone inside, Maybe, as I say, it's all inside. " Ronak said to Roshan with Bluetooth in his ear.

"That's right. But if we go to break the lock, the voice will come, man." Roshan said.

"Yes, but we do not break down the door. We are on the west wall of the circle and we have already placed in all four directions men. So who's in the West? "Ronak asked.

"I don't know everyone's names, One of the men on the terrace came in with say to open the door or the outside window as the windows are all sliders, If we open it high, it will open, "said Roshan.

So when Roshan asked a man from above to point, One student came to the west wall. So he gestured to his to open the window. So one student dared himself and later another gave him a cover. He ran up to the wall at speed and as soon as he reached it he became dizzy. That is, someone has to be able to. Keep it lightly open the window so that no one can hear. Then he opened the window and saw the movement and felt that everyone was hiding here. So everyone told him 'We are students of the hostel, we will get you out.' So if he got it all, he didn't know where to go now. So he reached the locked door and knocked a little. So there Ronak said lightly, 'First there is no one across the circle, there are only our men, jump and take it later. And yes all our men ball or slowly third And goes to the last fourth circle and Then finally the school building will be one left. I don't think there is anyone but maybe there is! We don't care '

"I'm saved, Hundreds are up here. It will take time, backup is needed. " A voice came from inside.

"We are, take everyone." Ronak said.

Students of both classes were taken to the front of the circle. There was a slight movement in the second circle and Ronak stood there without any sound. But someone came out of the third floor from the east side in the circle, So Ronke signaled not to shoot now. Let everyone come out first. Then do something.

So five came out. All who were defeated had guns in their hands and returned And the bullet runs to know the sound from somewhere. So no sound came. Ronak signaled to everyone that this would kill one, This will kill others. So five people arranged the gesture. He was then shot dead with a gesture. After completing the second circle in this way, the students going to the third circle appeared in one class and Nilesh went to the classroom to bring him in the second circle. This was Nilesh standing on the first floor while Ronak was standing outside in the class and chasing everyone in the second circle. There, in the second floor window, a terrorist dropped a graded bomb on the first floor window. But soon a student of the hostel shot him. Graded in the class where Nilesh was standing. They all came out. Nilesh had no time to leave until the bomb exploded. Ronak stood outside the class and was thrown out. Roshan and the other siblings erupted. But he looked like a terrorist and threw a bomb at him, so the hostel student was not judged.

Here Nilesh inside and Ronak outside.

....

Part 14 : (decision)

Ronak was thrown to the heights. Nilesh was in the room and was seriously injured. Bloody Nilesh fell and the four stages of the battle were over.

When Ronak got a little wake up, you had a ringing in his ear, He woke up and looked around. Roshan came running from a distance. Ronak's ears and nose were bleeding profusely. There was a wound on the eye as if something had been hit by a stone and blood was coming out from there. Roshan came and reached there and when he stood up he started banging his legs loudly, So Ronak screamed loudly. Now Ronak had no choice but to fall back, He just insisted that everyone should be saved now. So he did well by shaking his legs a little. Ronak went to the room with Nilesh and the whole room was filled with black smoke. (This is shown in Part 1 now.) There Nilesh took his last breath and found heaven. Ronak was furious. There was no end to his anger as he took responsibility for everything but Nilesh died.

(With three hours to go before the NSG arrives, the fifth phase of the war continues.)

"Roshan, listen a lot now." He spoke loudly and loudly. "Student coming in from all sides, keeping everyone backed up. If attacked. No need to kill a terrorist in hiding now. Directly visible and kill. As much as killed while running. No need to pity anyone anymore. Complete the fifth step, "Ronak said.

All backed up as they were told and came in from all around. Ronak said he would kill anyone who appeared outside the hostel with a gun while running.

Ronak himself was running forward. He took a small gun and confronted them And started firing. As Ronak approached the terrorist, he would fight with his hand without a gun and strangle him. All of a sudden everyone was wondering where the ghost of the Army was. Ronak was so angry that he decided to kill everyone. Like a monster, terrorist would die a miserable death without being forgiven. All those who were hiding in the class sent him to where had kill the terrorist and moved on. At last Roshan gave him his gun and all the weapons he had and went to fight. Two four six eight buses just had to be counted. In doing so, he completed all the circles and Ronak was declared the winner of the college. Everyone started screaming.

Now the school was left alone. But since it was a holiday at school, no one came, but maybe those people are hiding? But there was no hiding place. Meaning victory was won without NSG commando. Ronak could not save some people, Whose hand was behind this was left to be killed. As Ronak came on the road, college students and hostel students met their mom, dad and family, Nilesh's mom was looking at Dad Ronak, But Ronak shook his head and refused and started crying. Nilesh's family was there to cover him. But Ronak fainted because of the injuries. He was then taken to hospital. Ronak's brother and his family were present. He was treated well there. If it got a little better, I ran away to someone's house without asking. There was an old man sitting in the house. Going home, Ronak sat next to his uncle, the house would be like fifty crores.

"How are you sir?" Ronak said.

"You're Ronak's savior!" Uncle said.

"I told the police my brother and finally you knew there was going to be an attack. I got proof. You are a trustee!" Ronak said.

"Yes I am the trustee. Why what happened?" Uncle said.

"How many rupees did you eat, five hundred and sixty crores?" Ronak said.

"You know that. More than that." Uncle said smiling. "Then go with them." Ronke shot me in the head as he said.

Ronak's bravery saved many lives But if the trustee was living for money, he would have betrayed, Which resulted in the loss of many lives. India may have become helpless today, That the man inside was going to bring the terrorist. This is not a hostel attack, but an attack on a hostel terrorist. It's not hostel attack, it's attack by hostel student.

[All the characters created in this event are fictional.
Which is not a story about someone's life.
But where is the proof of bravery shown? Take note of which.]
Written by HEMILKUMAR P PATEL
THANK YOU.

www.ingramcontent.com/pod-product-compliance
Lightning Source LLC
LaVergne TN
LVHW050422160726
843469LV00041B/1202

* 9 7 8 9 3 5 6 1 0 5 6 9 0 *